Chuckle Bob's Great Escape

JEREMY STRONG

With illustrations by
Scoular Anderson

This is for small monkeys
wherever they might be found.

First published in 2013 in Great Britain by
Barrington Stoke Ltd
18 Walker Street, Edinburgh, EH3 7LP

www.barringtonstoke.co.uk

ISBN: 978-1-78112-215-0

Printed in China by Leo

Contents

1   The Great Escape   1

2   Jellyfish on the High Street?   9

3   The First Days   17

4   Giants!   25

5   A Nasty Surprise   32

6   Fever   39

7   That Crazy Chuckle Bob!   46

Chapter 1
The Great Escape

"Watch out! The monkey's escaped!" Mr Rush yelled at Maya, his young helper. Maya swung round in time to see the monkey leap on top of the parrot cage.

"Shut the shop door before he runs out!" Mr Rush was waving his arms madly. Maya didn't think that was a good thing to do. Surely it would scare the monkey even more? "Bad boy," said Mr Rush. He reached up towards the monkey.

"Mind he doesn't bite you," Maya warned him.

Mr Rush laughed. "He wouldn't hurt a fly, would you, Chuckle Bob? Come on down, you rascal."

Chuckle Bob banged his little fists on the parrot cage. This startled the parrot, who gave a loud squawk and tried to peck at Chuckle Bob's long tail. Chuckle Bob jumped off the cage in fright and landed with one leg in a fish tank. The tank wobbled and water slopped over the sides.

Chuckle Bob let out a cross squeak and leaped out of the tank. He grabbed a bird cage for support. It toppled over. The door banged open and the bird fell out into the fish tank. Maya grabbed the bird and got it back in the cage just as Chuckle Bob managed to pull another tank onto its side. The contents sloshed all over Maya.

"Urgh! It's cold! I'm soaking! There's a fish down my jumper!" Maya stood up and shook herself. "Urrgh!" Water flew off her arms and hair and a couple of fish fell out of one sleeve. Mr Rush helped Maya catch them all and pop them into a different tank.

They had just rescued the last fish when Chuckle Bob took another leap across the shop. As he jumped, he kicked the gerbil box into the rabbit pen. In an instant small creatures were running in every direction. Mr Rush and Maya scrambled to catch them. Chuckle Bob threw himself into the air, grabbed at a light shade and swung upside down, watching with great interest.

Mr Rush fetched a ladder and began to climb up. Chuckle Bob let go of the light shade. He landed for a moment on Mr Rush's head, then scampered down the poor man's body. Then he darted behind the dog pens.

The puppies yapped like crazy and tripped over each other as they raced round their pens. The birds flapped and squawked. Even the fish charged round their tanks like crazy submarines. The hamsters and mice got their exercise wheels to whirr round at supersonic speed. It was amazing they didn't take off!

Mr Rush banged his leg as he climbed down the ladder. "Ow!" he cried. "Chuckle Bob Jones, you are the most pesky monkey in the world! Come here!"

But Chuckle Bob had begun to enjoy his freedom. It was a long time since he had been able to stretch his legs. He clattered up to the top of the bird cages and sat just above the canaries. He looked down at Mr Rush and Maya with black, shining eyes and scratched an itchy cheek with one slim finger.

Mr Rush stepped back and sighed. "Pass me that ladder, Maya. I shall have to climb up again."

Mr Rush was halfway up the ladder when the shop door opened with a tinkle of the little bell. Chuckle Bob, Maya and Mr Rush turned to look at the door. A lady stood there, with a little white dog panting at her feet.

"Good afternoon," the lady began. "I would like to – EEK! Help!" She pointed at Chuckle Bob on top of the bird cages. "A giant spider!" The lady screeched even louder than the parrots in the shop.

Poor Chuckle Bob was scared of the noise. He whizzed through the air towards the open door. He landed beside the astonished dog. The dog yapped and snapped. It began a wild dash round and round the lady's legs, until she was tied up with the dog lead.

"Help!" the lady squeaked as she started to topple over. Mr Rush just managed to get to her in time to fling his arms round her and stop her falling.

Mr Rush held the lady up. The dog jumped up and down and yapped like crazy. Maya stood in a large puddle of water and stared at Mr Rush hugging the lady.

Chuckle Bob Jones took his chance and zoomed out through the open door into the big wide world.

Chapter 2
Jellyfish on the High Street?

Feet!

Legs!

Noise!

Crash!

Yell!

Scream!

Zoom!

Ow!

Huge hands tried to grab Chuckle Bob. Someone pulled his tail. Someone else snatched at his leg, but he pulled free. He showed his teeth, hissed and spat and tried to escape by climbing up a man's leg. The man hopped about on one foot and waggled the other leg in the air. Chuckle Bob clung on for dear life.

"Ouch! Oof! There's a hairy beast on my leg. Get off!"

The man shook his leg so hard that poor Chuckle Bob was thrown into the air. His long arms and legs whirled like crazy. When he came back down he landed on an old lady's head. She gave a screech that made Chuckle Bob's ears ring.

"Aaargh! A giant spider! A vulture! A buffalo! Save me!" The old lady screamed so hard that her false teeth shot out of her mouth. Then she went stiff with fear and turned white from top to toe. Chuckle Bob scrambled as fast as he could down her back to the ground. He jabbered in anger as he darted away. He was cross and fed-up with all these stupid, useless two-legged creatures around him. Where was the forest? Where were the tall trees? Where were his furry friends?

Chuckle Bob zigged and zagged between the flashing feet and legs. But instead of trees and friends, all he found were giant, roaring monsters. They screeched and honked as Chuckle Bob darted between the cars. He had never seen such fearsome, glittering beasts.

SKREEEEEEKKKKKK!! BANG!!

There was a tearing crash as two cars slid into each other. Chuckle Bob almost jumped out of his skin and ran even faster, his heart beating like crazy. He twisted, turned and leaped through the crowd. Behind him Mr Rush and Maya struggled to push through a crowd of excited shoppers.

"What are we doing?" asked one.

"There's an escaped tiger," was the answer.

"No, no, it's a kangaroo. I saw it jump," said someone else.

"It's a jellyfish," said another.

"A jellyfish? On the High Street? You're mad!"

"Who are you calling mad? You said it was a kangaroo."

Up ahead of the crowd a small, very scared monkey scampered up a lamp post. Chuckle Bob perched on the top as the crowd moved in below. The lamp post was surrounded.

"Now we've got him!" cried a man. "Come down! Come down!" He waved his baseball cap at Chuckle Bob. Maybe he thought the monkey would jump into it.

"I'm going to climb up and get him," one teenager said. "Here, you crouch down and give me a leg-up."

The man with the baseball cap bent over. The teenager climbed onto his back and grabbed the lamp post. He twisted his legs round the post and began to climb up towards Chuckle Bob.

"We'll soon have him now, the pesky thing!" That came from the woman who thought Chuckle Bob was a spider, a vulture, or perhaps a buffalo. (To be fair she didn't have her glasses on.)

Chuckle Bob looked down from his high perch at the climbing lad. Then he looked out over the town. In the distance he could see something green. Grass! Trees! Branches and leaves! Secret hiding places!

"Go on! Grab him!" the crowd yelled as
the lad reached towards Chuckle Bob. But the
monkey was too quick. He gave the biggest leap
he could onto the gutter over a shop. He clung
on for a second, and then he swung up and
was on the roof. A moment later he was racing
from one roof to another until he reached
the last building. Then he grabbed on to a
telephone line and swung hand over hand to
the telephone post.

Chuckle Bob dropped down to the ground
and jumped away through the bushes. The tall
grass closed around him until only the tip of his
black tail could be seen. It moved through the
grass like a super-speedy beetle.

The crowd fell back as they saw that the
monkey had escaped. Only Mr Rush and Maya
tried to follow. They didn't stop until they
reached the edge of the woods.

Mr Rush stared into the trees and shook his head. "We shall never find him now," he panted. "Poor Chuckle Bob."

Maya looked at Mr Rush. "Perhaps he'll be all right," she said. "He's a monkey! He can live in the trees."

Mr Rush gave her a sad smile. "Oh yes, Maya, Chuckle Bob will enjoy the trees. But there's no food for him out there. He eats bananas and oranges and things like that. And what happens when he meets a fox, or a badger, or even a weasel?" He shook his head sadly. "I hope somebody finds him. That crazy monkey!"

Chapter 3
The First Days

It was the end of summer and the days were long and warm. Chuckle Bob swung through the trees, happy at last. This was much better than any cage! His fur was glossy and thick. His eyes were bright with interest in everything around him.

All the first day he picked at leaves and poked his fingers into holes. He annoyed some busy ants. He found an old bird's nest and stuck it on his head like a hat. He wandered down a narrow path and came to a sunny clearing in the trees where rabbits were nibbling the long grass. He ran among them with his long arms stretched out and scared them half to death. (He was still wearing his hat.) What a great game!

Evening came and Chuckle Bob grew tired. He hunted around for his warm cage, but of course it wasn't there. He spent half an hour in a useless search for it and his pile of warm straw. Then somewhere deep in his brain an old memory lit up. He remembered how his family had slept when he was in the South American forest.

Chuckle Bob climbed high into a beech tree and began to pull leaves and twigs together. Before long, he had built a small nest to lie in. He curled up and drifted off to sleep, with his tail dangling over the edge like a furry bell-pull. He was lucky. The nights were not cold. Not yet.

In the middle of the night Chuckle Bob was startled by a loud hoot. He leaped to his feet in alarm and almost fell out of the tree. He stared into the inky darkness but he could see nothing. Then the ghostly noise came again, right above him.

TOO-WOO! TOO-WOO!

Chuckle Bob forgot where he was and took a step back into thin air. He made a wild grab at a branch to stop his fall and climbed back to his sleeping place.

The owl in the tree above was almost as surprised as the monkey and swooped away.

Chuckle Bob stared into the night for a long time, wondering what had made that awful noise. At last sleep came to him again.

Early next morning Chuckle Bob woke. His tummy growled with hunger. He needed food. He felt like he could eat an elephant, and he would have been very happy to have eaten the bowl of fruit that Mr Rush used to bring him every morning. But there was no Mr Rush, no fruit and definitely no elephant.

By mid-day the sun was high in the sky and Chuckle Bob's tummy burned with hunger. He was going to have to find food for himself. He looked at the trees and bushes but there were none that he recognised. He had no idea which ones might have fruit or berries he could eat. He searched around but all he found were some spiders and a few caterpillars. He put them into his mouth and chewed. Yuck! The taste made him squeeze his eyes tight shut. His face wrinkled up until he looked a hundred years old. He spat out the caterpillars as far as he could.

Chuckle Bob widened his search and at last he had a piece of good luck. He found a bramble patch. Most of the berries were not ripe yet but the monkey didn't mind. He picked away and his mouth was soon stained with juice. This was a lot better than squidgy spider stew or cruddy caterpillars.

When he reached the last bush he saw something even more interesting. The bramble patch was right beside an apple orchard! In a flash Chuckle Bob was among the branches, stuffing himself. He was a tidy eater – he even swallowed the cores. After a while he lay back on a broad branch and dozed in what was left of the day's sun.

That night Chuckle Bob returned to his nest tired, full and happy. He threw away his old bedding and built a fresh platform of leaves. Soon he was asleep and not even the hooting owl disturbed his rest.

Many more days like this followed. Every day he went to the same little orchard. He even found a few pear trees there. The puzzled farmer could not understand why the trees near the wood had so little fruit on them. He

never glimpsed the little monkey, steadily chewing away.

The farmer didn't even see Chuckle Bob throw an apple at him to make him go away. The apple hit the farmer bang in the back. He whirled round.

"What the …!" He scratched his head.

But Chuckle Bob was safely hidden among the leaves. If monkeys could laugh, Chuckle Bob would have been in hysterics.

The little monkey did not notice the leaves begin to fall and the days grow shorter. The weather was still warm and kind. But winter was coming and Chuckle Bob Jones had no idea what winter was, or how hungry he would be when the snow came. And he certainly had no idea that the winter months would bring out more starving animals – the big ones.

Chapter 4
Giants!

One October morning two children appeared in the wood. In fact, part of the wood was in their back garden. Daniel and Jessica often went there for walks. They loved kicking up the fallen leaves.

Chuckle Bob rested high in his tree and glared at the children as they passed beneath him. He didn't like humans very much. They were like giants to him and he had bad memories of the day he had been chased all over town. Then there was that lad who climbed up the lamp post and almost caught him. Giants were all bad, as far as he could see.

Now, if Chuckle Bob had kept quiet the children would never have spotted him, but instead he started to beat his chest and make loud "whoop-whoop" noises to scare them away.

Jessica looked up, her eyes wide with surprise. She grabbed her brother's arm and almost jumped out of her shoes with excitement.

"Look! A monkey! It's a monkey!"

They stared with open mouths while Chuckle Bob snatched up some twigs and hurled them down at them. Jessica giggled.

"He's funny!"

"I'm going to get him," Daniel declared. He strode towards the base of the tree. "We can take him home. He'd be brilliant! And we could take him into school. Everyone in my class would love him. And we could take him into the Head Teacher's office and shut the door and wait for Mrs Crossley to scream. I bet she would scream her head off."

"No she wouldn't," Jessica said. "Mrs Crossley isn't stupid and she's not afraid of little monkeys. Anyway, you'll never climb that tree. The branches are too high."

Jessica was right. (She most often was, which Dan found very annoying.) Even the lowest branches were just out of Daniel's reach, but Daniel was Jessica's big brother and he took his sister's words as a challenge.

"If you bend down I could stand on your back," he pointed out.

Jess sighed. That was typical Dan. He got to climb the tree while she got used as a human ladder. Jessica sometimes thought that being the oldest child must be the best thing ever. She had no idea that Dan sometimes thought she got all the treats because she was the youngest.

Jessica crouched down and Dan climbed up.

"Ow!" she squeaked. "You're worse than a rhinoceros! Hurry up!" Jessica stood up as Dan pulled himself into the tree with a loud grunt. He stood on a branch and grinned down at her in triumph.

"Told you I could do it!"

Jessica ignored him. "I bet you've got mud all over the back of my coat," she complained.

Chuckle Bob watched as Dan scrambled up the tree. His black eyes sparkled. What fun! He filled his paws with beech nuts and chucked them at Dan's head. *Bipp! Bopp! Bupp!* They bounced off without doing Dan any harm, but they were annoying. Dan tried to dodge them.

"Hey!" he cried. "Stop it! I only want to help. Come on, little monkey."

But Chuckle Bob hurled one last clutch of nuts at Dan and swung away, whooping with excitement. He vanished amongst the leaves. Daniel slowly returned to the ground.

"I almost got him," he said glumly. Jessica grinned.

"You've got a pile of beech nuts stuck in your hair," she told him. "And a big twig."

When the children got home they told their mother all about Chuckle Bob.

"It must have been a squirrel," Mum smiled.

The children insisted it was a monkey until Mum got cross and told them to stop arguing with her. Dan and Jess looked at each other. They couldn't blame Mum. After all, nobody would expect to find a real monkey hiding in the wood. But *they* knew it was true.

"We'll look for him tomorrow," Dan whispered to Jessica. She gave him an excited nod.

But before Dan and Jess could return to the wood several things happened to Chuckle Bob. They were not good things.

First of all, when he went to the orchard, all the fruit had gone. The trees were empty because the farmer had harvested all the apples that Chuckle Bob hadn't eaten. The brambles had all gone long before. Chuckle Bob rushed round the orchard chattering with worry and confusion but he found nothing. When evening came his tummy was still empty.

Winter was on its way, and it would not only bring the cold. It would bring hunger for all the animals, big and small.

Chapter 5
A Nasty Surprise

That night the weather changed. The air was sharp with cold and Chuckle Bob shivered in his nest. It began to rain. He had been rained on before but this rain was icy and hard. It poked its wet, freezing fingers deep into Chuckle Bob's matted fur. He crouched down, unable to find shelter. Leaves tumbled down and stuck to him.

Chuckle Bob was miserable. It was very dark and he knew he could not stay out all night in the rain. He left his soggy nest and slipped down to the ground to hunt for dry shelter. He splashed through mud and puddles. A startled rabbit fled across his path at high speed, eyes filled with fear.

Chuckle Bob stopped dead, his big ears trying to catch sounds through the noise of the rain. He felt something was close by. In fact, he *knew* something was close by, but he didn't know what it was. There was an odd, strong smell. Chuckle Bob sensed danger. His muscles stiffened, on red alert.

If it had not been raining, Chuckle Bob would have heard the fox. He would have smelled the fox. But the rain drowned everything.

There was a sudden snarl and a crunching snap of strong jaws. Chuckle Bob jumped up in utter terror, and sprang round to face the big creature. A pair of slit green eyes burned out at him. The fox crouched and leaped again.

Chuckle Bob yelped as it grazed one of his ears. He lashed out with his own tiny paws. The fox gave a shrill whine as Chuckle Bob caught him on the nose. Biff!

Now the monkey turned and fled, shooting up the nearest tree. Whoosh! Right to the top he went, while the fox set his paws against the trunk and snarled. He sniffed several times, and growled with anger. At last he peed right round the trunk before slipping away into the darkness.

Chuckle Bob clung to the branch and shivered with cold and fear. The rain came down like tiny arrows. The monkey stayed there at the top of the tree all night, too afraid to move.

Hours later morning arrived and a weak sun broke through the clouds. Chuckle Bob shook his soaking body. It had stopped raining, but it was still cold. An icy wind ruffled his fur. He had to set out to find some food.

All morning he wandered through the wood, on the hunt for food. He grew more and more hungry. His tail drooped behind him. At last he reached the edge of the wood and discovered a large garden. He trotted across the lawn. There was something colourful lying on the bird table. Something he had seen before. An orange!

Chuckle Bob hadn't eaten an orange since he had escaped from the pet shop. He jumped onto the table and chewed at the bright fruit until juice ran down his chin. Then he hauled up a string of nuts and cracked them open with his teeth. It wasn't much, but it was better than nothing.

Jessica was in the kitchen when she saw Chuckle Bob on their bird table.

"He's in the garden!" she yelled. "Mum, look! It really is a monkey. We told you it was."

Mum and Daniel rushed over to the window.

"Well I never!" cried Mum. "I'm so sorry I didn't believe you the other day. What on earth is a monkey doing in our back garden? Just look at the way he's gobbling up the bird food. It's not a good time of year for a monkey to be out in the wild."

Jessica tugged at her mother's sleeve. "If we put out some more food we might be able to catch him," she said.

"That's a good idea," Mum agreed. So they cut up some fruit and took it to the bird table. Chuckle Bob dashed away the moment the kitchen door opened. He chattered and whooped like crazy. But as soon as they went back indoors he came back. He was still very hungry. So he returned and he sat on the bird table as if he was King of the Garden. He ate everything the children had put out.

Chuckle Bob came back every day after that. The family would watch him from the kitchen table.

"It looks like that monkey is used to our garden now," Dad said one day. "I think it's time we tried to trap him. Then we can make sure he's well looked after through the winter. Maybe we can find out who his owner is. He must have escaped from somewhere."

Daniel frowned and went quiet. He liked the idea of trapping the monkey. But he didn't want anyone to find out who his owner was. Daniel's idea was that he and Jessica would keep the monkey. Forever. A pet monkey would be such fun. They could play games, like chucking beech nuts at each other.

Chapter 6
Fever

Every day after that Dan and Jess and their Dad set a trap to try and catch Chuckle Bob. First Dad put a bowl of fruit under a big box that was propped up with a stick. He tied a long piece of string to the stick. The idea was that Chuckle Bob would go for the fruit and Dad would pull the string. The stick would fall down, and bring the box down with it. Chuckle Bob would be trapped.

But Chuckle Bob was too clever for that. He looked at the box very carefully. Then he got a stick of his own and knocked the prop out of the way. When the box crashed down he went over to it, lifted the corner and ate all the fruit. He looked straight back at the kitchen window, where four faces were staring out at him. Ha ha ha! You could almost hear Chuckle Bob laughing.

"The cheeky monkey!" Dad smiled.

That was just the first of many traps that didn't work. But the weather was a trap that Chuckle Bob could not escape. Every day was colder than the one before. The snow came and laid its blanket of white across everything. It all looked new and very different. The woods weren't much like a South American forest at all.

Chuckle Bob sneezed and shivered in his nest. He wiped a small paw across his face. He was ill. He was used to warmth and sunshine,

not this awful cold. He huddled low in his hollow tree and tried to keep warm. Every day he grew weaker. It was a struggle to even get to the garden to eat.

"He's so thin," whispered Daniel one morning, as Chuckle Bob sat in the snow and chewed on a banana. "Isn't there anything we can do?"

"We can't help him unless we catch him," Mum said. "And he won't let us do that."

That afternoon the snow fell again. Chuckle Bob watched from his tree. By the time it got dark it had lined the edge of his hole until there was a thick, cold layer like half a front door. All through the evening it snowed, and on into the night.

Chuckle Bob's bones burned and throbbed with fever. His eyes were dull and half closed. He lay and listened to the mournful hooting of the owl. He heard the shrill bark of the fox as it stood and sniffed the bottom of the tree. Chuckle Bob's blood ran cold.

When morning came the snow had changed everything again. Chuckle Bob dragged himself onto a branch and gazed with watery eyes at the strange scene. He sat there for ages, trying to gather enough strength to reach the garden. He almost fell to the ground because he could not grip the icy branches.

At last he staggered out across the smooth white lawn of the garden. Daniel ran to his parents in alarm.

"Quick Mum, Dad! Look at him! He's dying!"

They stared out as Chuckle Bob tried to get to the pile of fruit they had left for him. Before anyone could stop her Jessica had grabbed her coat and rushed into the garden.

"Don't!" Mum called after her. "You'll only scare him away!"

Jessica stopped at the edge of the lawn. Chuckle Bob froze and looked at the small figure standing so still on the other side of the snowy garden. He didn't move. He could barely focus his eyes. Jessica held out her coat.

Mum shook her head as she watched from the door. "The silly girl's still got her slippers on!"

"Come on, monkey," Jessica whispered. "I won't hurt you." She took a step forward. She didn't feel the wet snow seeping through her thin slippers. Her eyes were fixed on poor Chuckle Bob.

The monkey crouched low, trembling with fear and fever. He was so thin! Jessica bit her lip and moved closer. She was desperate to catch Chuckle Bob and carry him into the warmth of the house. She had never been so close to him.

Chuckle Bob bared his teeth and gave a half-hearted snarl. "Grrrr!"

"Shush!" Jessica whispered. "Don't be so silly. I won't hurt you, little monkey."

Just a few more steps now. Mum, Dad and Daniel hardly dared to breathe as they watched. At last, Jessica was right beside the monkey. Their eyes were locked on each other.

"Go on, Jess," whispered Dan. "Go on. You can do it!"

Chapter 7
That Crazy Chuckle Bob!

Jessica knelt in the snow and put her coat around the trembling monkey. She lifted the bundle into her arms and walked back to the house.

Mum was already on the phone to the vet. He came out right away and was amazed that Chuckle Bob had survived for so long.

"It's a miracle he's still alive," the vet said. "He's a very lucky animal."

"Will he be all right?" the children asked.

The vet nodded. "Most of all he needs to be kept warm. I have given him a jab that will help him shake off that fever. He'll be alright in a few weeks. I know where he came from too. His name is Chuckle Bob Jones." The vet told the family about Mr Rush and the pet shop. Jessica's face fell. Dan gritted his teeth. He felt like punching something – anything.

"Oh," Jessica murmured. "Then he isn't ours after all."

Mum burst out laughing. "You two! You didn't think we were going to keep a monkey, surely? We have one already!" Mum pointed at Daniel. He scowled and turned bright pink. If Mum thought she was being funny, he could put her right.

Over the next week the children nursed Chuckle Bob. He grew stronger and stronger every day. Then the day came that the children dreaded most. Mr Rush called. They would have to face up to the fact that the monkey would be taken away from them.

Mum made Mr Rush a cup of tea and they all sat and watched Chuckle Bob explore one of Dad's welly boots. He kept climbing inside so that only his tail could be seen, waving out of the top.

"I'm amazed he survived out there for so long," Mr Rush kept saying. "He does look at home in that boot, doesn't he? I'm so glad he's all right."

When he had finished his tea, Mr Rush turned and picked up his coat. "Thank you so much for looking after him so well," he said. "I must be off now."

"Wait!" cried Mum. "Aren't you going to take Chuckle Bob?"

Mr Rush shook his head. "Oh no. I don't think that would be good for him at all. He is so at home here with you and you're better at looking after him than I am. He'd try to escape again, and you should have seen how much damage he caused last time! Besides, it's not much of a life, sitting in a cage, is it? He's got trees here – and welly boots! He'll always come back to you. He might stay away for a night or two in the summer, but he'll always come home to this snug, warm house and good food. I'm so glad he's found such a good place for himself. Cheerio, Chuckle Bob!" And Mr Rush left.

"Well," said Mum, glaring at her two children. Then a big smile burst across her face.

Chuckle Bob climbed out of the boot. He picked up a banana, peeled it and ate it. He did a sudden back-flip, whizzed up the curtains and hung from the very top. And for his final party piece he carefully placed the yellow banana skin on his head like a drooping star. He looked down at them all with sparkling eyes.

Mum shook her head. "That crazy Chuckle Bob!" she sighed.

Our books are tested
for children and young people by
children and young people.

Thanks to everyone who consulted on
a manuscript for their time and effort in
helping us to make our books better
for our readers.

More from *Jeremy Strong*...

The Ghost in the Bath
JEREMY STRONG

Luke is in a lot of rubble – sorry, trouble. He hasn't done his history project for Mrs Rubble. The last thing he needs is a ghost in the bath...

Can Ellie the ghost get Luke out of hot water?

Living with Vampires
JEREMY STRONG

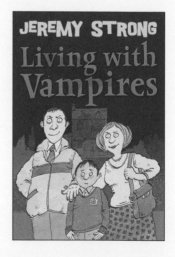

Kevin's a bit scared of vampires. Not scared they'll bite his neck. Or scared they'll drink his blood. He's just a bit scared they'll make a fuss at parents' night.

Vampires – they make *such* uncool parents.

Mad Iris

JEREMY STRONG

Mad Iris doesn't like the ostrich farm. She likes Pudding Lane School much better! But the men from the ostrich farm are hot on her trail...

Ross and Katie to the rescue!

Mad Iris Goes Missing

JEREMY STRONG

It's cup final week and Pudding Lane are all set to win. After all, they have Mad Iris as their Mascot. But someone else has other ideas...

Mad Iris is missing!